The Lost Plantation

Deborah Grant-Dudley

Also in this series

The Lost Castle

The Lost Cargo

This is dedicated to everyone who supported my first book. Whether you read the book yourself, bought a copy for someone else, followed my blog, shared a social media post or wrote a review (most especially if you wrote a review), you are wonderful. Thank you.

It is also for the warm-hearted, hospitable people of Costa Rica, who inspired every event in this book.

Contents

Curubande, Costa Rica
April 1850

The wooden chair fell and clattered noisily on the floor as Andreas rose unsteadily from his table. His dark eyes blinked in the hazy light, and he raised a rough hand to his weary head. The room had only a few lanterns yet seemed bright to him. It must be time to go home, he reasoned. He was not used to rich food and drink but that night was a celebration. He had just returned from delivering his first coffee harvest to Puntarenas on the pacific coast.

He had returned via Ciudad de Guanacaste, the nearest city, and was almost home now. The journey had taken him two weeks but he had an empty oxcart and a full purse to show for it. His elderly parents, who were not in the best of health, had left the plantation in his hands. He had planted the land with coffee, and the crop had grown well in the rich soil. He planned to visit them soon and show them the money he had earned.

His ox, Principe, had been left to rest in a nearby field while Andreas had enjoyed a fine meal. The Hacienda, or plantation house, was the last rest stop on the way back to his own small plantation. The farmer kept a close eye on the purse hanging from his waist, although after several days travelling on the oxcart wearing the same clothes, he did not look like someone worth stealing from. His shirt was rumpled and the hems of his trousers were covered in dust from the road.

Certainly the family who owned the Hacienda seemed unlikely to steal from him. The house was huge, with at least thirty steps leading up to a veranda at the front, and a large courtyard with views across the expansive plantation at the back. There were handmade clay tiles on the roof and floor, and the tables and chairs had been built to last. These people had made a good living from farming sugar cane but the recently introduced crop of coffee had brought new opportunities.

Over the last 20 years, many farmers in the region had started coffee fincas - small family-tended farms. Some had expanded and taken on employees, until a new class of wealthy 'coffee barons' had started to emerge. Andreas dreamed of joining them. One day he would own a beautiful Hacienda, and travellers would gaze in envy at his home and plantation. The payment for his harvest was the first step on that road.

Not only had he been paid a very large sum, but the money was in brand new gold Escudos, the first Costa Rican coins to have the coat of arms commemorating his country becoming a sovereign republic - an independent country, not ruled by anyone else. Although Andreas's family was mestizo - a mix of native Chorotega Indians and the more recent Spanish settlers, he considered himself entirely Costa Rican. The coins gave him another reason to celebrate so he had taken a glass of sugar cane rum with his meal, which was increasing his feeling of tiredness.

He stepped outside, placing his feet slowly on each step before turning towards where he had left Principe. Finding the sun had already set and the field was now in near darkness, he decided to come back for the ox in the morning. He took the lantern from the cart and started walking home.

The path was fairly straight but on one side there were low-hanging tree branches, and on the other was the river bank, so he took care on his journey. The low croak of unseen frogs, the incessant whisper of cicadas, and the urgent gushing of the river accompanied him.

After a short while, he heard a different sound; a padding of large feet perhaps. He looked back but it was dark, and the glow from the lantern was not bright enough to see if there was anyone there. Fearing a thief, he kept his hand on his purse. A few minutes later, he heard the sound again, more distinctly this time, which meant it was moving closer.

He looked back a second time, not to see who was there but to let the person following him know he was aware of their presence. For a moment, he thought he glimpsed two glowing red eyes behind him but he knew he must have imagined it. There were red-eyed tree frogs in the rainforest all around but they were small and hard to see. They also hopped so did not make the sound of footsteps.

"Hola," he called out.

No-one responded so perhaps it was not a person. It certainly wasn't a frog. This was a much larger animal, possibly a jaguar, and the sound seemed to be coming from the path directly behind him.

Andreas began to walk faster, as his heart rate increased and his breath became shallow. He continued moving forward, as fast as he could in the darkness, looking back every few seconds. This was a mistake; in his weary state, he stumbled on the uneven path and fell onto the slippery bank.

His desperate grappling with the grass failed to slow his descent. Twigs and stones scraped his skin as he slid downwards, and panic took hold. He tumbled into the cold, black river and felt a chill as the water quickly passed through his clothing.

The Rio Colorado was not at its full depth during the dry season but as it flowed from the mountains down towards the lowlands, gravity created a fast-moving current that pulled him away from the bank. There were rocks in the river and Andreas knew that without help he would probably not survive. But it was late and there was no-one around.

"Ayudeme!" he shouted in Spanish, water splashing into his mouth. 'Help me'.

Hearing no reply, he repeated his plea, more urgently, "Ayudeme! Ayudeme!"

His voice did not carry far above all the other sounds of rushing water, nocturnal animals and people in the Hacienda. No-one called back to him. A dog heard him though, and began to bark loudly to attract attention. Andreas tried to swim towards the animal, knowing it was his best hope, but made little progress in his heavy, wet clothes. He could see the lights of the Hacienda receding as the river carried him away from anyone who could save him.

It is over now... my life is over, he thought, as his limbs became stiff with cold.

Taking a final look back up the river, he saw a light-coloured shape moving in the distance. It appeared to be coming towards him through the dark water. As it got closer, he could make out it was a boat. The dog must have succeeded in alerting someone.

A voice called out to him, but he couldn't hear what it said. Someone was coming, that was all that mattered. Andreas used the last of his energy to stay afloat until he felt a strong hand grab his arm and pull him to safety.

For a moment, as he lay shivering in the boat, all he could do was breathe. When the shock started to subside, his first thought was to check his soaked purse, which was now empty. He silently berated himself for his carelessness before realising he should be thankful he was still alive.

"Gracias," he mumbled to the barely visible figure rowing him back to the bank.

His heart was still thumping so loudly in his chest, he could only hear part of the reply but he thought he made out the words, "El Cadejo."

Andreas had heard the legend of El Cadejo, the supernatural dog who follows lone travellers at night. He put little stock in these stories although he knew others believed them to be true. The stranger must have heard the barking and jumped to this improbable conclusion. Andreas said nothing. He was not about to argue with the man who had saved his life.

Once safely back on dry land, Andreas thanked the stranger again. He looked around for his other rescuer but the dog had disappeared into the darkness.

One

Creatures in the Forest

Travelling 5000 miles west has added seven hours to Cameron Barnes' day. He feels like it has added seven days. He runs a hand through his brown hair, knowing he looks a mess.

His dad looks worse; he needs a shave and seems less tall than usual after 11 hours squashed into his seat on the plane. That's OK for him, but Cameron is 14 - it matters what he looks like.

It is light outside although his body is telling him he should be going to sleep now. But it is too bright, and too hot.

"This was a great idea of your mum's, wasn't it?" Mr Barnes asks, using a hand to shade his dark brown eyes from the sun.

Cameron's mother has been sent to train some employees in her company's Costa Rica office. She works for a big technology firm with offices around the world. Cameron would not usually describe her as cool, but she has added an extra 10 days to her stay so he and his dad can join her for a holiday and he has to admit that is fairly awesome. He is not planning to tell anyone that, though. Thinking your mum is cool is not cool.

"Ask me when I've had some sleep," he jokes.

There is a transfer bus to the hotel. Cameron bags a window seat; even though he is tired, he doesn't want to miss a moment of this.

It is thankfully only 45 minutes to the coast, and a very scenic journey. There is no visible development, which seems odd in a country with big technology firms. Everywhere Cameron looks, he just sees plants and trees; it doesn't look like anyone lives here. There are hardly any houses, and the few he spots are just tiny one-story buildings. The gardens are, without exception, larger than the houses. Most of them have one or more dogs relaxing in the shade. There seem to be more dogs than people.

"Where is everybody?" Cameron asks.

"There are only around five million people in Costa Rica. That's not a lot of people for the size of the country," Mr Barnes explains. "Most of them live in cities so it is just farmland and countryside here."

They reach the hotel, which looks more like a palace. It is on the pacific coast and there is an outstanding view of the sea. A man and woman in traditional white Costa Rican clothing greet them with warm smiles, and usher them into the hotel. A man in hotel uniform brings over a tray of brightly-coloured drinks, while another brings in their bags.

They collect the keys from reception and find their room, where Mrs Barnes is waiting.

"Oh, you're here - I'm so pleased to see you!"

Mrs Barnes rushes over to hug them both as soon as the door opens. She has been staying in the room on her own for a week but greets them as if she hasn't seen them for months. She looks just the same as the last time Cameron saw her. Her hair is still sandy brown, her skin is still light. She has clearly been at the office most of the week, and not enjoying the sunshine as Cameron had secretly suspected.

The adults chat about the flight and the hotel while Cameron looks around the room. It is very large with a king size bed and a double bed, which he gets to himself. The beds are both in the same area, with no partition, which could get awkward. He guesses it would have been very expensive to book an extra room.

They get changed and go to the hotel restaurant for dinner. There are burgers, pizza, fried chicken and chips alongside the rice and beans and fried plantains.

"Why is so much of the food American?" Cameron asks.

Before anyone can answer, he realises most of the guests are speaking with American accents.

"Oh, right. We're near the U.S.A.," he says.

They have a light meal and go to bed immediately afterwards. Cameron is used to getting undressed in the privacy of his own room and changes into his pyjama shorts in the bathroom. The second his head hits the pillow, he is asleep.

The next morning, Cameron wakes up early because of the seven hour time difference. He checks his watch and finds it is only three o'clock. He creeps out onto the balcony to avoid waking his mum who has started to get used to the time difference and is able to stay asleep for longer. It is not completely dark although there are no lights around. There is already a faint glow from the sun which is due to rise in around an hour. He can just make out where the hotel gardens end and the forest reserve begins. He sits in one of the chairs, feeling comfortably warm despite the early hour.

As the sun starts to rise, he sees movement in the trees straight ahead. There are so many leaves it is hard to make out the shape of the animals but he thinks they might be squirrels. The balcony door slides open and Mr Barnes joins him. Cameron puts a finger to his lips to let his dad know they need to be quiet, and they watch together.

"I think they must be some kind of monkey," Mr Barnes says.

"They are small though, like squirrels," Cameron replies.

"Costa Rica has many types of monkey. I haven't heard of any squirrels that live here," Mr Barnes counters.

Cameron sees one of the animals run along the ground.

"They run like squirrels," he says.

"But their tails are narrow, like monkeys."

"They are staying on all fours. They don't sit like monkeys do."

"They might do, you can't see the ones in the trees properly."

The debate peters out because whatever they might agree on, there is clearly a correct answer and neither of them knows what it is.

By this point, they are getting hungry and

wonder when breakfast opens. Cameron has some cereal bars in his bag and opens the door to go and fetch them.

"Good morning," murmurs Mrs Barnes, reaching for her glasses.

"Sorry, didn't mean to wake you."

"That's OK; I woke up at three o'clock on my first day."

"We went on the balcony so we wouldn't disturb you. There's a great view."

"Yes, there's a lot of wildlife out there. Did you see the squirrel monkeys?"

Two

Basketball and Dogs

Apparently, there is no such thing as a free holiday. Mrs Barnes has to go to a corporate family day and she expects Cameron to come along.

"There is a basketball court for the kids, and a buffet," she says, encouragingly.

Cameron can't see a way to get out of this, since his mum's work is the reason he has been able to come here.

"Sounds great," he says, trying to smile.

He throws his swim shorts back in the suitcase, and dresses in sports shorts, a t-shirt and trainers instead, while his mum organises a taxi.

An hour later, they enter the city and the driver makes his way along busy roads edged with offices and shops until they reach the community centre. They go inside and make their way to the hall. They are quickly surrounded by strangers and this makes Cameron feel a little awkward.

Lots of people come over to say hello to Mrs Barnes and to meet him. He is surprised how many of them already know his name. He hopes he will not need to remember all of theirs.

Someone shouts the basketball game is about to begin. Cameron heads over to the court and volunteers to take part. Everyone is assigned a position, given either a blue or yellow vest to wear, and paired up with someone around the same size to mark.

Cameron is marking a girl, about his age, who introduces herself as Joselyn. She is wearing very bright make-up. The deep orange eyeshadow is an unusual colour but it emphasises her hazel eyes. Her hair is golden brown, just a shade darker than her skin. What really catches his attention is her vivid purple lipstick; he thinks his mum calls that colour 'fuchsia'. He tries to stop staring at it when he realises Joselyn is speaking.

"My mum works in the Liberia office. She mentioned your mum was working over here for a while."

She puts on a blue vest, while Cameron dons a yellow one.

Once the players are in position, and everyone else has gathered round to watch, the game begins.

An athletic-looking boy in bright blue trainers from the blue team and a tall boy wearing a proper basketball kit from the yellow team are selected for the 'jump ball'.

The referee throws the ball into the air and the two players jump up and try to hit the ball in the direction of their basket. The blue team gets the ball and the boy in blue trainers tries to pass it to Joselyn, but Cameron blocks the pass and steals the ball.

"Nice move," Joselyn says.

Cameron smiles, but he has taken his eye off the ball and Joselyn steals it back.

"Nice distraction technique," he replies.

Joselyn shoots, the ball hits the backboard and everyone watches as the ball falls through the hoop. She runs around in celebration, leaving Cameron unmarked. He grabs the ball, dribbles past a girl in a pink t-shirt, and passes to a spiky-haired team-mate, who takes a shot from the three point line. The crowd cheers as it lands in the basket.

"I guess I should keep my eye on you," Joselyn says, laughing.

The blue team have the ball now, but not for long. The tall kid from the yellow team manages to grab it, and Cameron moves down the court ready for a pass. Joselyn stays close despite his efforts to shake her off.

The boy passes to him and he catches the ball but can't pass to another player because Joselyn is in the way. He dribbles, then swerves away from her to make enough space to take a shot. It goes wide but a girl with long black hair is close enough to the hoop to knock it in.

After fifteen minutes the teams change sides. The blues get a basket almost immediately and it is not long before Joselyn redeems herself with an impressive on-target jump shot. The crowd cheers.

After a bit of a scuffle with the long-haired girl, the tall kid gets the ball and passes to Joselyn. Cameron is ready for her and extends his arm above his head to block the shot. She has to pass to the pink t-shirt girl.

The spiky-haired boy takes the ball from her, but she plants herself between him and the basket. Cameron moves closer to her, blocking her movement and allowing his team-mate to dribble around Cameron and get free.

He takes the shot. It hits the rim and rolls. Everyone holds their breath for a second until it falls into the hoop. Another cheer goes up from the crowd. No-one seems to mind too much which side is in the lead.

The match ends with a respectable score for both sides, and the onlookers applaud vigorously. Cameron and Joselyn shake hands. Cameron is feeling sweaty from all the running about in the heat and wonders how Joselyn's make-up stays on. All the players head for the drinks table for some much needed refreshment.

A small group of young people who didn't take part in the game are standing near the refreshment tables. They all look cool and dry, and Cameron wishes he had brought a different top to change into.

"So what do you think of Costa Rica?" Joselyn asks, between gulps of water.

"Well, the countryside is so green and full of farms and forests, I wasn't expecting the city to be full of offices and technology firms, or people who speak English."

"It didn't used to be like this. Do you know the history of the Guanacaste region?"

Cameron shakes his head, and she continues.

"600 years ago, this region was populated by the Chorotega tribe who had relocated from Mexico. They lived simple lives and used cacao beans for currency. Then Spanish people came and tried to take over."

"I'm guessing that didn't work out so well for the tribe?"

"It didn't work out so well for the Spanish, either. They expected to find gold here, but we don't have any in this region. They had to grow crops to survive so they tried to take the indigenous people as slaves to work on their farms."

"And they met resistance?" Cameron guesses.

"They found smaller numbers of people than they were expecting. Some of the Spanish people arrived infected with European diseases that were fatal to the people already living here and that reduced the population further. It was a really hard time for everyone but eventually the people mixed. Everyone was growing their own food and not making much money. Then coffee arrived in Costa Rica."

She pauses as if he should know what this must have meant for the country. He drinks some more water to avoid having to comment.

"Many people started small coffee plantations," Joselyn continues. "But only a few became very rich. Basically until quite recently, most people here were poor."

"What happened recently?"

"Eco-tourism has become very popular. Everyone learns English at school now because there are so many tourists from English-speaking countries. Most of the tourists are from the US but there are more coming from the UK every year, and other European countries where English is the second language. Education is free and lots of people go to university, so a lot of people here have skills that companies in other countries need and now we speak the language many of them use, too."

"I don't know if I will go to university; it costs a lot of money in the UK."

"I'm really lucky I don't have to worry about that. You want to get some food?"

Cameron's stomach rumbles.

"That sounds like a good idea."

Joselyn points out different snacks.

"These are patacones, these are tamales..."

Not being familiar with those terms, Cameron takes a handful of tortilla chips and some fruit. After eating, they take some coffee and sit outside, in the shade of a big tree.

"So what are you going to do while you are here?" Joselyn asks.

"My mum has booked a trip to the rainforest. We are staying overnight. It probably sounds boring to you, I'm sure you've been there loads of times, but we're excited to sleep in a cabin in the forest."

"Oh, I love the rainforest! I've never slept there - that will be amazing. My family used to live in the countryside. Actually, they owned a coffee plantation, a really long time ago," Joselyn replies.

"Used to? What happened?" Cameron asks, sensing a story behind this.

"They fell on hard times and had to sell the land. I don't know much more than that. It really was a long time ago - the 1850s, I think."

She frowns a little as she considers this, then her usual cheerful expression returns.

"It all worked out for the best. It would be nice to know a little more about my family history, but I'm happy here."

Cameron senses there is more to this story, that Joselyn isn't ready to tell him. A cute brown dog walks past, with no owner in sight, reminding him of all the other dogs he has seen.

"There are a lot of dogs here. They must be very popular," Cameron says.

Joselyn smiles and leans close to him, and he wishes again he had brought a clean T-shirt.

She says, "Let me tell you a story."

Three

Folklore and Mystery

"Sometimes when people go out at night, particularly if they are alone, on a dark, empty road..." Joselyn pauses, wide-eyed to build suspense. "They might feel like someone, or something, is following them. Sometimes they hear footsteps. Sometimes they look back and see red eyes in the darkness. They might hear the breath of a large animal just behind them. Very few people see what it really is that follows them home."

She sits back, satisfied she has piqued Cameron's curiosity.

"And what is it?" he asks.

"It is El Cadejo: a huge dog, black as night, with red eyes... that follows people in the dark!" She pauses again, and Cameron stifles the urge to laugh.

"What does it do to them?"

"It protects them and makes sure they get home safely," she replies.

Cameron laughs at this, relieved Joselyn's dramatic retelling hadn't been serious, and she begins to laugh, too.

"Do you have any other folklore here?" Cameron asks.

Joselyn thinks for a moment.

"There is La Careta Sin Bueyes - the Oxcart without Oxen. It's the story of an oxcart that appears in the early hours of the morning. There is no ox pulling it - it moves by itself. People say that if you see La Careta sin Bueyes, it means someone close to you will die soon."

"That is a horrible story. I wonder why someone made that up."

"It probably came from Europe. Apparently when there were plagues, people who died in the night would be collected early in the morning and carried off in a cart."

"Well, we don't have that story where I live."

They are both quiet for a moment, and can hear some music which someone has put on inside. A family with two small children comes out of the building. They find their own space under the tree.

Joselyn speaks again, "There is a sad story from the tribal days of the area my family comes from. The legend tells of the princess Curubanda, who was the daughter of the Curubande chieftain. She is said to have fled from her father to the Rincon de la Vieja volcano to be with her lover, who was part of an enemy tribe. But her father followed her and threw her lover, Prince Mixcoac, into the crater of the volcano. Mourning her loss, she became a recluse, living out the rest of her life alone. They named the volcano Rincon de la Vieja, which means 'old woman's corner', because Curubanda lived there, all alone.

"That really is sad," Cameron agrees. "Do you have any cheerful stories?"

"Not really. We have a witch monkey, called La Mona, who screams from the tree tops."

"Great. I'll try to avoid that."

"It is probably just a story somebody made up to stop their children wandering off. The children hear a howler monkey, think it is La Mona and go back where it is safe."

"I don't think I've heard any howler monkeys yet," Cameron says.

"You will know when you do," Joselyn replies, laughing.

"I did see some squirrel monkeys."

"You are lucky then. The Central American Squirrel Monkey is a vulnerable species. There aren't many around. When are you going to the rainforest?"

"We have a trip tomorrow."

"You might see spider monkeys too, then."

Cameron laughs at this.

"You have funny names for monkeys here," he says. "Spider monkey, squirrel monkey, howler monkey..."

"We have funny names for birds too", Joselyn explains. "There is the umbrella bird, the bell bird, the whistling duck... Then there are the snakes like the green parrot snake and the shovel-toothed snake. But I think the best named animals are the bats; I like the tent-making bat and the hairy-nosed bat."

Cameron giggles. He finds her very funny. She starts to laugh, too.

When they have calmed themselves, Joselyn says, "Some weekends I go to the beach with my friends. You could come with us if you aren't busy on Saturday."

Cameron is surprised that someone who lives here and has all her friends around would make the effort to include him in her plans.

"That's kind of you. I'm not sure what I'll be doing after the rainforest trip, but if you give me your number, I'll let you know if I can come."

On the way back his mum says, "Are you glad you came? You wouldn't have got to play basketball today if you hadn't."

"No, I would have had to settle for water volleyball in the hotel pool. That would have been a disaster!" Cameron jokes.

"Well, I think that girl was glad you were there. You were talking for quite a while."

"Yeah, she was telling me about her family history. It was really interesting. I might read up on some stuff when we get back," he says, hoping his mum's interest will be diverted by what he is going to learn, and that she will stop asking questions about his new friend.

"I've been thinking about all the things we can do together while you are here,' Mrs Barnes says. "There are museums, hikes, classes, and of course there are the trips I've already booked. I've got some information about museums we can visit in a day, if you'd like to choose which ones you're most interested in," she continues, with a hopeful expression.

"You know, I sort of promised Joselyn I'd help her with something," Cameron replies, trying to think of an excuse to get out of spending the whole 10 days with his parents.

"Oh, what's that?"

"What's what?"

"What are you going to help Joselyn with?"

A tone of suspicion has entered Mrs Barnes voice and Cameron knows he needs to come up with something right now or his mum will be upset with him. And if there's one thing that's worse than spending 24 hours a day, for 10 days, with your parents, it's doing that after you've upset one of them.

"Well, it's her family history," he says. "They used to own a coffee plantation and she really wants to find out what happened to it. It's very important to her."

Mrs Barnes eyes him warily for a moment.

"I suppose it would be nice for your dad and I to have a bit of time to ourselves."

Back at the hotel, Cameron feels he has to prove the veracity of his story. He gets his tablet out of the safe and does an internet search to see if he can find any information about a coffee plantation near Curubande. There is nothing relevant online.

It appears the full story has been lost to history as well as to Joselyn's family. But that little detail isn't about to stop Cameron Barnes. Not when there is family bonding to avoid.

Four

The Forest at Night

A disappointingly large group of people are waiting for the coach to the rainforest. Cameron stands to one side and views his fellow passengers.

There is an older couple looking relaxed and tanned, with a bag stuffed full of everything they might possibly need for the trip. They look like they are frequent travellers, probably retired. Next, there is a young couple who look very excited and keep checking the road to see if the bus is coming yet, as if they don't do this sort of thing on a regular basis. They might be on their honeymoon, Cameron thinks. Then there is a mum and daughter who appear to have only decided to book the trip since arriving in Costa Rica, as their clothes and footwear are not remotely suitable for the rainforest.

There is also another family of mum, dad and son, like the Barneses. The boy looks about 10 years old, and is wearing a T-shirt with a smiley face on it.

Cameron imagines his parents will try to befriend these people and he will have to spend the next two days with an annoying younger kid following him around.

He tries to distract them from talking to anyone by drawing attention to the activities board.

"There are lots of sports here," he says.

"There's a 'Welcome to Guanacaste' meeting, too," Mrs Barnes says. "Learn about the geography, history, culture and language of the region," she reads aloud. "We should all go to that."

"Yes, that might help us with finding our way around," agrees Mr Barnes, always thinking of practicality.

Cameron groans silently.

"Or we could go to beach volleyball instead?" he suggests.

"Maybe," Mr Barnes replies. "I was thinking table tennis might be fun."

"They have aerial yoga!" Mrs Barnes exclaims.

Fortunately the coach arrives before Cameron has to think of a reason not to accompany his mum to that class. The guide gets off to meet them. He is a tall, young man with dark, spiky hair. He tells them his name is Enrique.

The younger boy starts practising saying his

name, "Enrique, Enrique, Enrique..."

Cameron sighs; this could be a long trip.

Everyone boards the coach and settles into their seats for the journey. Enrique switches on the microphone and talks enthusiastically about every minor point of interest they pass by.

After several hours they see the tall cone of the Arenal volcano rising up ahead of them. The boredom of the journey is immediately replaced with excitement as they all feel they have almost arrived.

"Thousands of people used to live in the towns of Tabacon, Pueblo Nuevo and San Luis around Arenal volcano but had to be evacuated when it erupted in 1968," Enrique explains. "There is a lake there now that provides electricity from hydropower."

Eventually, they reach the cabins. The annoying kid gets off the coach and puts on a cap that says 'Cuba' on the front, as if letting everybody know that he thinks of himself as an expert traveller. He comes over to introduce himself to Cameron, who wishes he wasn't the only other young person on the trip.

"Hi, I'm Arthur," the boy says, in a confident tone.

"Cameron," is all he gets in return.

Everyone collects their keys and an information

sheet, and sets off on the many winding little paths to find their cabin. Although there are around twenty cabins on the site, they are spaced well away from each other with plenty of trees all around. They are all several minutes walk from the reception and restaurant buildings.

The Barnes's cabin is a small wooden building with a large front porch which has an amazing view of the volcano. Inside there is one bedroom with two double beds, and a bathroom containing a toilet, sink and shower. There is nothing else in the whole cabin. It is surrounded by large-leaved trees and plants in a variety of bright colours, and has a solar panel outside for hot water.

"There is nothing to do here," Cameron says.

"You can sit on the porch and look at the volcano," says Mrs Barnes. "It's very peaceful."

"A peaceful volcano, that doesn't sound quite right," Cameron replies.

Mr Barnes explains, "Arenal erupted almost constantly for years until 2010. A show of red lights could be seen almost every night, but it is resting now. There are no fireworks anymore."

They have a little free time before their first group activity. Cameron looks at the information sheet and sees there are hot springs. He remembers the hot springs, called onsens, in Japan, where people bathe naked. The information for this trip had said to pack swimwear though, so he thinks it is probably OK.

"We could go to the hot springs," he suggests to his parents.

"Good idea!" says Mrs Barnes.

A few minutes later, they are standing in just swimwear on a very, very hot floor. Cameron can't stand still without his feet hurting and has to get in the water. It feels much more comfortable in the natural pool. There is plenty of room and he lays on his back and floats on top of the hot water.

The pools are surrounded by brightly-coloured tropical trees. Green iguanas wander around on the ground and birds call to each other from their hiding places in the branches. After half an hour, they feel totally relaxed and not at all ready to head back to the cabin and get changed for the next activity - a night-time walk through the rainforest.

There is just time for a cup of tea, made using energy collected by the solar panel, before setting off for the meeting point.

They join the rest of the group, and collect torches from the rainforest guide, a small man dressed from head to toe in green, called Eduardo.

He says, "You must stay on the path, as there are streams and lakes around the forest. If you see something interesting, just call out and we will all stop and look."

A little further on, he stops and asks them, "What do you think is the most dangerous animal in this forest?"

The guesses include jaguars, and snakes, but he shakes his head to these.

"Ants?" asks Arthur.

"Ants?" repeats Cameron, in a condescending tone.

"That's right!" Eduardo says. "Army ants are ruthless hunters who swarm on, and kill, any animal they find, even much larger ones."

Cameron feels something crawling on his leg and knocks it off, quickly.

The torches don't shine very far and it is hard to even make out the trees. The guide has a much better torch which he uses to direct their attention to animals in the forest. They see tiny green tree frogs, hiding on leaves, only their bright red eyes giving their locations away.

They hear large bull frogs calling to each other, in their deep croaky voices. Arthur copies them.

They see lightning bugs, which flash in one

place, then another and another, like magic.

Arthur stops the whole group every time he sees an insect. He finds cicadas, which Cameron pretends he isn't interested in. He has heard them but never actually seen them before, but doesn't want Arthur to know that. He expected them to look something like grasshoppers but they actually look more like giant bumblebees without the cheerful yellow stripes.

There are also spiders and millipedes, which he is more familiar with, and katydids that look like elongated beetles with long antennae. There are millions of insects in the rainforest and Cameron is bitten by unseen ants every time they stop. He is starting to find Arthur really irritating.

Something leaps across the path in front of him and makes him jump. It is just a tiny tree frog. A rustling close by in the undergrowth makes him jump again. He points his torch in the direction of the sound but can't see the animal he knows is there.

The guide aims his torch towards a tall tree and they see a brown furry body hanging upside down in the upper branches. It is a sloth, moving very slowly through the tree, one arm or leg at a time. A stubby triangular tail protrudes from one end of the body, and there is a cute little beige-coloured face at the other end.

"This is a two-toed sloth," Eduardo tells them.

"Did you know sloths are very slow moving in the canopy but can swim quite fast?" Arthur asks, popping up unexpectedly beside Cameron and making him jump again.

"Really?" Cameron replies, wishing he did not find this interesting.

"Sometimes they fall in water and have to be able to get out quickly so they don't get eaten by predators. Like the caimans that live here."

"We're walking around in the dark in a place that has caimans?" Cameron asks, with concern.

Arthur laughs, assuming Cameron is joking.

"We should be friends," says Arthur. "I don't know anyone here, and you don't know anyone here, so we should do stuff together!"

"Actually, I already have a friend here. Her name's Joselyn and I'm helping her find out about her family's plantation. They lost it in the 1850's and we're investigating what happened."

"Oh," Arthur replies, "That sounds really interesting. Maybe I could help?"

"Over here, everyone," calls Eduardo, quietly, waiting at the side of the path for the group to gather round him.

They have reached a lake but Cameron can barely make out the water in the darkness. Even with his torch, it just looks black and empty.

"Look around the edges of the water," Eduardo instructs them.

A sweep of his powerful torch reveals several pairs of eyes just above the water line, which is very disconcerting.

"These are caimans," Eduardo tells the group.

Cameron can't see any other part of their bodies, but he understands they are large reptiles, like crocodiles, with powerful jaws and large teeth.

"Perhaps someone in your friend's family was eaten by caimans and the rest of the family had to move away for their own safety," Arthur whispers.

The cabin is now starting to seem a lot more welcoming.

Five

The Daylight Trail

The group is back on the coach for a daytime trek through a different part of the rainforest. They will be passing close to Curubande, and Cameron hopes to learn something about the plantation there.

Enrique is their guide again today. Mr and Mrs Barnes, and the older couple, are trying to listen to the information he is giving out over the microphone. Everyone else is chatting over him or simply trying to ignore him.

The road runs parallel to the volcano range for much of the journey, which provides stunning scenery for the passengers. Cameron looks for signs for any plantations they may pass by. If he can find a plantation name, he may be able to work backwards to link it to Joselyn's family. There are very few signs and none that relate to a plantation.

"This is the Cordillera de Guanacaste," Enrique says, pointing to the volcano range.

Cameron gives up on the sign idea and instead tries to work out which of the white streaks above the dark peaks are trails of steam released from the volcanoes and which are passing clouds.

It is a shorter journey this time and they soon arrive and meet their rainforest guide, Mariana. She is small, with short, wavy light brown hair and is dressed in grey cargo trousers and a green polo shirt. Cameron is worried if he doesn't pay attention, he may lose sight of her. She explains she has been trained to help them spot animals, as many of the forest inhabitants are asleep during the day, which makes them harder to find.

The group follows Mariana along a path through bright green, tall trees. The branches of each tree are growing through gaps in the neighbouring trees, and there are even climbing plants growing up the tree trunks. Even though the sun is very strong, it is cool and shaded in the forest.

"It looks very different in daylight, doesn't it?" the frequent traveller lady asks Cameron.

"It's nice to be able to see any predators before we trip over them," he jokes, pleased to have someone to talk to, other than his parents, and of course, Arthur.

"It sounds like anything we see will be asleep!"

the frequent traveller man joins the conversation.

"Well, we should be able to get some good photo's today, then," the lady answers. "They won't run away if they are asleep, will they?"

Cameron laughs. They seem like nice people.

"What's your name?" the lady asks him.

"I'm Cameron."

"We have a grandson about your age, Cameron," the man replies. "I'm Bill, and this is Linda."

Mariana stops, and the group gathers around her as she points to a sleeping sloth, very high up in the tree tops. It looks like a large round fur-ball, with greyish-green colouring, and no discernible head, tail or legs. It doesn't look much like the creature they had seen the previous evening. It reminds Cameron a little of Mariana.

"That's a three-toed sloth," Mariana says. "Its limbs are curled around a branch so it won't fall out of the tree while it is sleeping. That is why it looks like a ball shape. If you stand over here you can just make out its head, with the dark band around its eyes."

Everyone shuffles round to try to see the sloth's face, and take a photo. Cameron uses the zoom function on his phone's camera to get a closer look as it is hard to make out any features from so far below. He can't see the toes clearly enough to count them and guesses the type of sloth has been determined from the colour of its fur instead.

They set off again, stopping a few minutes later to look at a lizard hiding in a tree. It is brownish-green and almost invisible against the leaves.

"I think I would have walked right past that if Mariana hadn't been here," Cameron says, impressed with her observation skills.

"It's a lot harder to see the animals than I had anticipated," Linda replies, taking a photo. "I'm not sure I'll know what is in that picture, when I get home!"

The next stopping point is a more easily identifiable sight: a copse of banana trees. Each tree has a huge hand of bananas reaching up towards its long flat leaves.

"You may see whole plantations of these trees. Bananas are one of our most popular exports, along with coffee," Mariana explains.

Cameron remembers Joselyn's family's plantation and wonders if it may have been replanted with a different crop. It seems the most likely alternative crop would have been bananas. Maybe he should be looking for a banana plantation instead of a coffee plantation!

The group follows Mariana as she loops back towards the start of the trail. She stops and gathers everyone round again.

"Can anyone guess what animal is sleeping in this tree?" she asks, with a smile, knowing this is a difficult question.

Everyone stares into the tree. Some of the group walk around, trying to see what Mariana is looking at.

"There it is," says Arthur.

He proudly points towards a sliver of dark brown fur, barely visible above a thick branch. The leaves obscure the majority of the body but a small foot with long toes can just be seen.

"It is too low in the tree to be a sloth, plus it has too many toes," Arthur says, doing his best to examine what little he can see of the creature above his head.

"Some kind of monkey?" offers Bill.

"It is not a monkey..." teases Mariana.

"I can't see any feathers, so it isn't a bird," Arthur continues. "It appears to have fur, so it isn't a reptile..."

"Is it a porcupine?" asks Mr Barnes.

"Well done," Mariana congratulates him. "It is a

porcupine!"

"How did you work that out? You can't even see any quills from this angle," Cameron says, surprised.

"Well I knew porcupines live in the rainforest - it said so, in the guidebook."

"Does anyone have any questions?" Mariana asks.

"Are there any plantations near here?" Cameron asks.

He knows this is not exactly the sort of question she meant but he may not get another opportunity to speak to anyone from this area.

"There are some banana plantations the east and some coffee plantations to the south," she replies, politely.

Everyone thanks Mariana and heads back to the meeting point, where Enrique is waiting with a cheery smile. Arthur appears at Cameron's side, once again.

"The rainforest used to be cut down for plantations but now the government is working with private landowners to reverse deforestation. They can earn money by planting native trees around their fields, or even returning abandoned fincas to their natural forest state," he says, authoritatively.

"What's a finca?" asks Cameron.

"A farm. That's what they are called here."

"Why didn't you just say farm, then?"

"Oh, maybe that's what happened to your friend's plantation. They could have moved away so it could be turned back into part of the forest."

Cameron hopes the answer isn't that boring, but it would explain why he has been unable to find the plantation. He gets back on the bus and stares out of the window not bothering to look for signs now he knows the plantation is probably either east or south of his location, and he is currently travelling west.

Six

The Forest in the Clouds

Back on the coach, Enrique takes the microphone and reminds everyone they will be travelling to the cloud forest after a break for lunch.

"It is only a short journey to the restaurant but please look out of the window on the way as there are some interesting things to see in this area. Over to your right side, you can see some steam in the distance, at the base of the volcano. This is a geothermal energy plant. It produces electricity from the heat of the volcano."

Everyone looks towards the drifts of steam, way off in the distance.

"And in a moment you can see small rope bridges above the road," Enrique tells them.

Cameron leans against the window. Sure enough, one of these bridges soon comes into view. It is too small for a person to use, and doesn't look very sturdy.

"These are monkey bridges," Enrique explains, enthusiastically. "They allow monkeys to travel unrestricted through the forest without having to come down onto the ground where they are vulnerable. This way, the people can have roads to get to wherever they need to go, without trapping the monkeys in a small area of forest."

Shortly after the monkey bridges, they stop for lunch in a restaurant that is completely open at the back to give a fantastic view of the neighbouring river. It is a very traditional place with a tiled floor and wooden tables and chairs.

As soon as everyone has chosen a seat, the waiters bring food to the tables. There are tortilla chips, a dip made of beans, omelette, corn on the cob and a selection of sauces.

"Try this one," Bill says, passing a bottle to Cameron. "That's what the locals have."

Cameron puts some on the side of his plate and dips a tortilla chip in it, before putting the chip in his mouth.

"Mmm, that's nice," he says.

"It's got a bit of a kick," Bill replies, laughing.

Cameron dips another tortilla chip in the sauce, but then the heat from the first one starts to fill his mouth. His tongue feels like it is on fire. He puts the chip down and has a gulp of water.

"Might take a bit of getting used to," he says, starting on his omelette instead.

When everyone has finished, the waiters come round again to see if anyone would like ice-cream for dessert. Cameron accepts gratefully, still not quite recovered from the hot sauce.

By the time they reach the cloud forest, he is feeling fine again, until Enrique shows them the first of a series of hanging bridges they will be using to traverse the forest. The bridge is made of metal and has been placed in the tree canopy, about 20 metres above the ground. It is very long and the other side is not visible through the clouds. The braver members of the group start to cross. The bridge sways as people walk on it, and Cameron feels a little nervous.

He waits for the people in front to start crossing, then leaves a small gap before stepping carefully onto the bridge, holding the handrail as he walks. His parents walk behind him, careful not to cause unnecessary movement. Cameron tries to keep his eyes on the back of the group in front but they are moving faster than he is, and one by one they disappear into the mist.

"Hi," Arthur says, suddenly appearing beside

him.

Cameron gasps, and grips the handrail more tightly. Arthur leans over it to get a good view of the trees below.

"Are you sure that's safe?" Cameron asks him.

Arthur notices he is clinging to the rail.

"Are you scared of heights?" he asks.

"No, I'm just not sure how safe things are here," Cameron replies, wishing Arthur would find someone else to bother.

"Did you know the Monteverdi Cloud Forest Reserve has around 2000 plant species, over 400 types of bird, and more than 100 species of mammals?" Arthur says.

"No," Cameron replies.

He wishes he felt comfortable enough to move at a quicker pace so he could put some space between himself and Arthur. They pass tall trees with other plants growing on their trunks and branches.

Arthur says, "They are called epiphytes. There are ferns, orchids and bromeliads here, that all live on the trees. It's too dark and wet on the ground. Look!"

Cameron glances over the side of the railing. It is dark underneath the canopy but he can just make out a small stream, weaving between the thick trunks.

"There are giant tree ferns too," Arthur continues, pointing to a strange looking tree with a large mop of leaves on the top.

"Gather round," calls Enrique. The group have stopped and are waiting for the stragglers to catch up.

Everyone moves towards the middle part of the bridge, where Enrique is standing, making the bridge sway more vigorously. Cameron clings to the rail.

"You may notice you are starting to feel a little damp," Enrique says, with his trademark cheerfulness. "That is because we are up in the clouds. Water from the clouds collects on the leaves of the upper branches of the trees and slowly drips down to the shorter plants below, so no rain is needed, only the clouds. That's why it's called a cloud forest."

He gives everyone a few seconds to look around before continuing.

"You may also notice the air is thinner due to the high elevation. If you are finding it harder to breathe, please take your time. We will all meet up at the end."

As the group starts to move again, Cameron waits at the back to avoid Arthur, who is now moving forward at a steady pace. Once Cameron is sure Arthur is not going to rejoin them, he begins walking again. By the end of the first bridge, he is starting to get used to the height and the eerie mist. Once on the path, there is dense forest on both sides, and they pick up the pace to keep the back of the group in sight, slowing a little when they reach the next bridge.

By the fourth, and longest bridge, the group has completely disappeared in the clouds. Mrs Barnes is breathing heavily.

"I think I need a little rest," she says, stopping and leaning on the handrail.

"Well, you picked a good spot. We might not be able to see much ahead of us, but if you look this way, the view is fantastic," Mr Barnes says, pointing over the side of the bridge, where the treetops are relatively clear of mist.

Cameron spots a hummingbird flitting from tree to tree, and points, careful not to scare it away by speaking. His parents watch with him and they share a quiet moment, amazed by this tiny green bird hovering in mid-air.

Their attention is soon diverted by something dropping from another tree. Leaves are shaking but initially they can't see what is causing the movement.

Watching closely, they wait until a brownish-grey creature that looks like a cross between a monkey and a cat, jumps from one branch to another. They remain still and silent until the animal disappears once more into the cover of the leaves.

The remaining two bridges are crossed more quickly. Excitedly, Cameron catches up with Enrique and tells him about the animal they saw.

He says, "That is an olingo. They are arboreal."

"Arboreal - that means they live in the trees, right?" Cameron checks.

"Yes. They are fairly common in the cloud forest but they sleep during the daytime and only come out when it is just starting to get dark. You are lucky - if you were at the front of the group, you would have missed it."

Cameron silently thanks Arthur for making him want to hang back. He rejoins his parents and relays what Enrique has told him.

"An olingo," repeats Mr Barnes. "I've never heard of that."

"I can't believe it," Cameron replies, stunned.

"I know, it's amazing, isn't it?" Mrs Barnes says, proudly. "I can't wait to tell everyone back home we've seen an olingo."

"Yeah," Cameron says. "I was sure it would be

called a monkey cat!"

Seven

The Market of Wondrous Things

Having got nowhere with his informal investigation, Cameron is texting Joselyn for more background information. He reasons she must know something that will help uncover the history of her family's plantation.

Hi Joselyn.
I was thinking about your
plantation story.

Hi Cameron!
What were you thinking?

Do you have any maps
or documents that say
where it was?

59

We don't have anything like that. Sorry.

Anything with even a partial address?

Just somewhere near Curubande.

What about the owner's full name? I might be able to look it up from that.

My mum just calls him my Great Great Great Grandfather Andreas. There should probably be a few more Greats than that...

Out of ideas now.

Want to go to the craft market today? There's a bus that goes from near your hotel.

OK.
See you there soon.

"I'm going out for a bit," he says as he leaves the room.

He doesn't allow his parents any time to ask questions. He doesn't want them reading anything into him going to meet a girl.

He stops at the concierge desk to find out where he can catch the bus for the craft market. The stop is just up the street, so he's surprised to find there aren't any other tourists waiting there.

The bus comes along in a few minutes. It looks very old and makes a lot of noise. Not having bought anything yet, Cameron has to pay with a note. He gets a lot of unfamiliar coins as change.

He looks around wondering how he will find the right place to get off. Maybe lots of people will get off at that stop, he thinks. The other passengers all look Costa Rican and seem to know where they are going. For some reason this makes him feel even more uncertain.

It is an uncomfortable but thankfully brief journey. Several passengers get up to leave as the bus pulls over and Cameron joins the back of the line, checking with the driver that this is the market before getting off the bus. He assumes the nod and smile means it is the right place.

Almost as soon as his feet touch the pavement,

he sees Joselyn waiting for him. She waves enthusiastically as he heads in her direction.

"Hi," he says, happy to have found her.

"It's good to see you," she replies, in her usual friendly way. "The market's just in here."

The market is a large, single-storey hall filled with stalls, where many different artisans are displaying their work. There are lots of people milling around looking at all sorts of goods.

"Wow, these are bright," Cameron says, eyeing some woven fabric bags.

"This is our traditional way of making fabric here. There are lots of different designs but they all have different colours mixed in, like our people!" Joselyn explains.

The next table has paintings on display and they stop for a moment to admire the colourful scenes of cattle, macaws, butterflies and tree frogs.

"Muy bien," Joselyn says.

The artist, an old man watching them casually from behind the table, smiles at her.

Further along they find a large pile of wooden boxes, stacked according to size. At the bottom is a heavy-looking large, plain box for storing blankets and other household items. On top of that is a medium sized box with a carved design, partially obscured by a smaller box. At the very top there are tiny jewellery boxes with beautiful inlaid designs of flowers.

The next stall catches Cameron's attention, as it has wooden sculptures of the local wildlife, displayed in neat lines. There are turtles, sloths and crocodiles. He picks up a crocodile and looks at the tiny bumps covering its back, and all the tiny teeth.

"Made by hand," the man behind the table says.

"These must have taken a long time," Cameron replies.

He carefully places it back on the table and inspects a small sculpture of a tree with a tiny sloth hanging upside down from its branches. The sloth has three carefully carved toes on each foot, and a little face.

Next he looks at a turtle with a honeycomb pattern carved on its shell. They are all more special than the usual tourist souvenirs.

"I like the sloth best. What do you think?" he asks Joselyn.

"I think I like the turtle most. It's so cute," she replies.

Cameron checks the price of the turtle. It costs a lot but he can see the care and skill that has gone into making it. He buys the turtle, paying with a note. His wallet is full of coins now.

"Gracias," he says to the stall-holder.

"Pura Vida," the man replies.

"That means 'good life'. He wishes you health and happiness," Joselyn explains.

"Here, this is for you," Cameron says, holding out the turtle to Joselyn.

She says nothing but touches his hand and smiles in a way that makes him feel like he's done something amazing, and not just bought a little thank you gift for his only friend in the whole country.

They continue walking around the hall. There are stalls selling practical things like chairs and bowls, so there are local people browsing as well as the tourists who have stopped en route to somewhere else. They have to wait to pass people in places but eventually make it all the way round and arrive back where they started. It is lunchtime and Cameron knows his parents will soon start wondering where he is but he doesn't want to go back to the hotel yet.

"Is there somewhere we can get something to eat here?" he asks, adding, "unless you have somewhere else you need to go."

Joselyn checks her watch.

"OK."

They find a little cafe nearby with a few chairs outside. They get a bowl of bean soup each and sit on the chairs outside, watching people come and go.

"My Grandma lives near here. I'm going to her house this afternoon to make tortillas with her for dinner. It's a tradition - I've done it since I was little," Joselyn says.

"That sounds like a nice thing to do together. I usually walk the dog with my Grandma."

"Oh, my Grandma has a dog, too!"

"Of course she does. She lives in Costa Rica, doesn't she?" Cameron jokes.

They finish their soup and Cameron looks around awkwardly. He still needs to find where to get the bus back to the hotel.

"You could come and meet my Grandma, if you like," Joselyn offers. "I'll show you how to get back to the hotel from there."

"OK, I'll just text my mum," he says, keeping his head down so Joselyn won't notice his smile.

Eight

The Grandmother's Tale

Joselyn's Grandmother's bungalow has been painted light green and is almost invisible amongst the surrounding trees. Joselyn calls out something in Spanish as she opens the door. The inside of the house is sparsely furnished and decorated in neutral colours. It feels like a calm place, for a moment at least.

A smiling lady in a wheelchair comes into the hall. She has wire-rimmed glasses, wiry black and grey hair, and is wearing an apron over her clothes. Accompanying her is a small brown and white dog of indeterminate breed, who starts running around frenetically.

"Hola, Joselyn," the Grandmother says, in an affectionate tone.

"Esta mi amigo, Cameron," Joselyn tells her Grandmother, before leaning down to kiss her on the cheek.

She turns back to Cameron to complete the introductions.

"This special lady is my Grandma Rosa."

"Hola," Cameron says, and receives a warm smile from Rosa in return.

"And this special dog is Giannina," Joselyn says.

She tries to stroke the dog's head, without much success, as Giannina is too excited about the visitors to stand still.

"Hola, Giannina," Cameron says, holding out his hand.

She bounds over to him for a cuddle, and he is happy to oblige.

Joselyn says something else in Spanish that Cameron doesn't understand, and Rosa turns and makes her way into the kitchen.

"We'd better wash our hands," Joselyn tells Cameron. "I've told my Grandma you're here to help with the tortillas."

"Oh, er, I'm not sure how much help I'll be," Cameron replies.

"Don't worry, it's easy."

They wash their hands while Rosa fetches a large tin and a small box from the worktop. Joselyn puts on an apron, fills a jug with water, and hands

Cameron three bowls and three spoons from a cupboard. They each arrive at the kitchen table with their contribution. The table is clear except for a basket of oils and sauces in the centre. Cameron hopes there will not be any hot sauce involved today.

Joselyn distributes the bowls and spoons, placing one of each in front of each person. Rosa pours some flour from the tin into her bowl without measuring, and passes the tin to Joselyn who does the same.

"First we add the flour," she says, passing the tin along.

Cameron pours very slowly, trying to add exactly the same amount to his bowl.

Next, Rosa takes a pinch of salt from the box and drops it into her bowl. They each copy her. She then makes a dip in the centre of the flour and adds some water, again without measuring. Joselyn does the same, and Cameron copies as closely as he can.

Finally, Rosa reaches for a bottle of olive oil from the basket and pours a small amount into her bowl, before passing the oil to Joselyn who copies expertly.

"Now, we mix it together," she explains.

Cameron again tries to copy but it is very

difficult to add the right amount of oil without a measuring jug, or the years of experience the other two have.

"Bueno, bueno," Rosa says encouragingly.

Joselyn and Rosa begin mixing the ingredients. This part seems straight forward. Next Rosa begins sprinkling flour around the table. Cameron is not entirely sure what is going on now but joins in the flour throwing when she hands the tin directly to him.

Rosa and Joselyn pick up the dough with their hands and slam it down onto the floury table. Pushing their bowls aside, they begin pressing down on the dough to flatten it out, then folding it back into a lump and pressing down again. This goes on for a minute or two. Cameron follows, glancing at the others frequently to check he is doing the right thing. They stop suddenly and sit back.

"Is that it?" Cameron asks.

The lumps of dough don't look like tortillas to him.

"We have to wait a little while now. This is the time when my Grandma likes to tell stories."

"Maybe she could tell me about the plantation?" Cameron asks.

Rosa understands the word 'plantation' as it is

similar to the Spanish word. She wipes her hands on her apron and starts talking in Spanish. Every now and then she pauses so Joselyn can translate.

"Grandma says she moved away from the city because she doesn't work now so doesn't need to be in such a busy place, but she wanted to stay close to us. Her family have lived in Liberia for a long time, since her great, great Grandfather Andreas lost all his money and had to move to the city. He had a coffee plantation in the hills near Curubande. He could have been a rich, powerful man but he was careless and lost all his money and had to sell the plantation."

"She seems to be saying more than you are translating."

"Yes, she says a lot of things that aren't exactly right. She gets things confused. You know, the date of this thing, the person who did that thing..." Joselyn shrugs.

Rosa continues talking, having no idea what her granddaughter just said.

"She's saying Andreas used to make beautiful oxcart wheels. Would you like to see one?"

"This was what he did in Liberia?" Cameron asks.

Rosa nods, understanding the name of the city,

if nothing else.

She shows him to another room where there is a huge wooden wheel displayed on the wall. It is beautifully painted in a colourful pattern of leaves radiating from the centre. It looks very old; some of the paint has flaked off, but it is still an impressive sight.

Rosa starts to speak in Spanish again.

"That is an oxcart wheel," Joselyn translates. "Traditionally, everything was transported by oxcarts, so they were very important to the people here. They would decorate the wheels of their carts with beautiful patterns, like this."

"Muy bien," Cameron says.

Rosa is happy with this and squeezes his hand for a moment, before returning to the kitchen to continue the cooking.

This time, the dough is broken into two sections, then flattened into thin round discs. Cameron is surprised to see his tortillas look just the same as the others. Joselyn collects the tortillas and takes them to the hob to fry them. She fries one tortilla at a time, flipping them over at just the right time to achieve a light golden colour. She has clearly done this many times before.

Once they are all cooked and have cooled a

little, she places two in a paper bag and hands them to Cameron to take back to the hotel.

A clock on the wall starts to chime; it is five o'clock.

"I'll show you where the bus stop is," Joselyn offers.

"Adios," Cameron says to Rosa.

"Adios,' she replies, "Pura Vida!"

They talk about Rosa's story as they walk.

"Do you think Andreas gambled his money away or was tricked out of it?" Cameron asks.

"I know my Grandma told me stories about a plantation when I was little and it always sounded like he lost it through poor management. But I'm not sure Andreas even owned the land. He might have just worked there."

"But if he did own it?"

"It's possible he was tricked out of it. There were a lot of businessmen trying to expand their farms at that time. Some people were getting very rich from growing coffee then, so it's possible someone found a way to steal the plantation. Andreas was a young man from the country; he probably wouldn't have known how to protect himself from ruthless businessmen."

"So he could have been tricked by a coffee

baron, expanding their operation," Cameron muses.

Joselyn smiles at his use of the new phrase.

"Maybe I'm being too hard on him," she says. "I'm assuming he was a gambler or really bad at managing his finances and I don't know that."

"I could look into well-known coffee barons from that time," Cameron offers.

"You don't need to find out what happened to the plantation, you know. I'm fine not knowing. It's not like he was the president."

"But it's history, and I like history," he replies. "I like puzzles, too."

He leaves out the part about wanting to do something that gives him breathing space from his parents. He is not sure his friend will understand.

The bus arrives and they say goodbye. Just as Cameron steps onboard, Joselyn remembers something.

"I do know the name of the plantation," she calls out. "It was La Plantacion en las Nubes!"

Nine

The River of Watchful Eyes

"It's too early," Cameron moans, pulling the sheet over his head, as Mrs Barnes opens the curtains.

The room is filled with light even though it is only 4.15 in the morning. A boat trip on the Tempisque river is planned for today, and apparently the wildlife is easiest to spot early in the day.

"I hardly got any sleep. Those noisy howler monkeys didn't stop for hours," he continues.

"Don't they make a strange sound?" Mr Barnes asks. "How would you describe it? It's not a howl, really. More of a wail, would you say? Or is it a moan?"

Cameron doesn't answer. It is clearly too early for describing animal sounds.

"We are leaving in half an hour, whether you're dressed and fed, or not," Mrs Barnes says, placing a cup of coffee and a day-old slice of banana bread on the table beside him.

"We don't get a proper breakfast?" Cameron asks.

"The restaurant doesn't open until seven," Mrs Barnes explains.

Cameron drags himself out of bed and eats the banana bread, which still tastes good even after a night in a hotel room. He would love a long, hot shower, but there isn't time so he has to make do with the coffee to wake him up.

Fifteen minutes later he is dressed, prepared and mostly awake. They head down to the front of the hotel. The coach is already waiting and other bleary-eyed people are making their way there too. It looks like a smaller group today. Just Cameron's family, another family with three children, and... as he enters the coach, Cameron sees Arthur and his family sitting at the front. He heads towards the back. It is too early for that much conversation.

When everyone is on board, they set off for the river. There is a different guide this time - an older man with grey hair, called Felipe. The first hour of the journey passes quietly, except for a few people yawning, then Felipe starts to share his stories.

"Years ago, this road was just a track, used by people on horseback or oxcarts. When we first started taking tours to the river, we had to take a very long route because there were no good roads here. Then the sugar factory wanted a way to reduce their waste, to be more environmentally friendly. Some of the waste they produced was molasses and the sugar factory donated molasses to surface this road. We are driving over molasses right now," he explains, smiling at all the surprised faces.

Now he has everyone's attention, he continues, "The river sometimes floods this area in the rainy season. Someone in this village we are passing through now was once trapped in his house for two days because there was a crocodile outside his front door. There was no way for him to get out of his house without going past the crocodile, so he just had to wait inside until the water receded."

The funny stories help the time pass more quickly, and they soon arrive at the river, and head down some steps to the boat. It is a long white boat, open at the sides, but with posts supporting a roof. On the way, they pass a large grey iguana lounging in a tree, with its legs hanging over the sides of the branch. It doesn't move at all while everyone walks past.

Arthur is waiting for Cameron, who has no intention of stopping to chat.

"Costa Rica has the fastest running lizard in the whole world, which is called the Spiny-tailed Iguana," Arthur says.

"That one doesn't look like it goes very fast," Cameron replies, still walking.

Arthur's family find a spot near the guide at the front of the boat; Cameron takes a seat right at the back. Mr Barnes raises his eyebrows.

"We will get better photos from here," Cameron says.

He waves his arm in an arc to demonstrate the unhindered view behind the boat.

"A few safety points before we start," Felipe says. "You must keep your hands inside the boat at all times. The crocodiles are wild and may bite a person if they are in easy reach."

Cameron quickly pulls his arm back inside.

"Please don't stand up while the boat is moving," Felipe continues. "You could fall in."

"Good advice," Mrs Barnes says, with a worried expression.

The boat pulls away from the jetty, and almost immediately they see an American Crocodile just a few metres away on the bank. It is about five metres long, with grey scaly skin, and very large jaws.

"That's a lot of sharp teeth," Mr Barnes

whispers. "I hope he isn't hungry."

Felipe speaks again, "The river is low because it is dry season now so crocodiles can be seen clearly on the banks. They are harder to spot in the water."

He points towards a small protrusion in the water. Everyone looks over, and one by one they gasp as they make out its eyes, and realise it is the top of a crocodile's head. The animal is watching them, with its whole body under water where it can't be seen.

Looking around, they spot more and more of these little lumps sitting just above the water, until they realise the river is filled with crocodiles. Some are only a few metres away. Cameron shifts uncomfortably in his seat, but there is nowhere else to go now he is in the boat.

Arthur begins counting aloud. "One... two... three... four... five... six... seven..."

The boat moves past the first group before he can finish.

"There is a large population of crocodiles in this river, because there is plenty for them to eat here," Felipe explains.

As they make their way along the river, Felipe points out tall birds lurking amongst the trees. These are night herons, darkly-coloured to be almost invisible in the night time.

There are also rough-skinned iguanas and lizards that look like little dinosaurs watching from the banks. Cameron tries to pay attention but finds his eyes straying back to the water, searching for crocodiles.

"There are sometimes pumas here, too," Felipe continues. "You probably won't see any, but that doesn't mean they aren't there!"

The boat stops so Felipe can help the group spot howler monkeys; dark shapes high up in the trees. Cameron listens for their distinctive call but they are quiet now, saving their fearsome noises until dusk.

A loud roar coming from the front of the boat makes him jump.

"Arthur!" call Arthur's parents in unison.

"That's what they sound like," Arthur retorts.

"Their sound is more like a loud groan," Cameron says, remembering his dad's earlier question. "It is definitely *not* a roar."

A blue heron flies past, stunning everyone, including Arthur, into silence, with its intense sky blue colour. Like the night herons, its colour is camouflage so its prey won't see it coming, but it is dazzlingly beautiful, none the less.

There is far more wildlife than anyone was expecting to see on one trip, and judging by the happy faces across the boat, no-one is regretting the early start now.

Soon though, it is time to head back. The captain reverses the boat to turn around. Felipe walks to the back of the boat to check there are no dangerous animals hiding nearby. Finding nothing to worry about, he signals to the captain, who brings the boat right up to the edge of the bank.

Sitting at the very back, Cameron is really close to the bank and looks around warily in case there are any crocodiles Felipe missed. He doesn't see any crocodiles but he does see something else; it's a small, dark, rounded shape sticking out of the mud. He checks the bank again, there are definitely no crocodiles. He scans the lower tree branches - no pumas either.

He knows he should keep his hands inside the boat but it is so close; it is literally right next to him. His parents are looking forward and wouldn't notice if he picked it up. Felipe has returned to the front of the boat and can't see him either. He hears a change in the engine noise as the captain puts the boat in gear to go forward. It is now or never.

He reaches out and grabs the object like

lightning. He slips it into his pocket as the boat moves away from the bank and starts back towards the jetty. With a pounding heart, Cameron looks back once more to the completely empty riverside.

On the bus journey back, Cameron is less successful at avoiding Arthur, who sits directly in front of him. He immediately turns around and tries to engage Cameron in conversation.

"I think all the wildlife here may contribute to it being a blue zone, don't you?"

Cameron sighs audibly.

"What's a blue zone?"

"You don't know what a blue zone is?" Arthur asks, raising his eyebrows. "A blue zone is a place where people live longer than everywhere else."

Once again, Cameron wishes he wasn't interested, and does his best not to pay attention. He takes the coin from his pocket while no-one is looking and wipes it on a tissue. He is disappointed to find it has the same coat of arms as all the other coins he has from Costa Rica.

He turns it over. It is darkened from being in the mud a long time and harder to make out the picture on this side. He needs to wash it to find out which coin it is but it doesn't seem like anything worth risking his arm for. He puts it in his wallet with all the others, and resists the temptation to shake his head at his own stupidity.

Arthur is still talking relentlessly.

"I liked the story about when the Tempisque river flooded and that guy got trapped by a crocodile!"

Something about this gnaws at Cameron.

"The river flooded.... do you think that happens to all the rivers here?"

"I don't know. Why do you ask?" Arthur replies.

"Just wondering," Cameron answers.

He is wondering whether Curubande is next to a river, that could have flooded and destroyed a coffee plantation.

He gets out his phone and looks for a map of the region. Curubande is near the middle, right next to the Colorado river.

Ten

The Obligatory Coffee Tour

Cameron really wants to find out what happened to Joselyn's family's coffee plantation before he goes home. He figures the best way to learn about coffee plantations is to go to one.

"Is there enough time left on this trip to go on one of those coffee tours?" he asks his parents, as they get ready to go to breakfast.

"We don't have anything planned for today or tomorrow," Mrs Barnes says. "We thought we might need some rest after the last few days."

"There is a desk just in front of the hotel where you can book day trips," Mr Barnes suggests.

They stop by the desk on the way to breakfast. The coffee tour is running that day and there is space for three more people in the minibus.

There is just time for something to eat before the pick-up time. Cameron is glad of a proper breakfast in the hotel restaurant, and fills up on pancakes, fruit and cereal.

It has been so hot every day that Mrs Barnes has taken to carrying sun cream and a bottle of water with her at all times, so they are ready to go. They arrive at the meeting point as the minibus pulls up.

The guide is a young man called Antonio. The small group takes their seats on the bus, and Cameron is happy to see that Arthur is not among them. The journey passes peacefully, and he is happy to just relax and enjoy the view from his window. He doesn't even put his headphones on. He nudges his dad as they pass through a village and he spots one of his favourite sights.

"Look, there's a football pitch. I heard football is popular here."

"I'm not sure how seriously they take it though," Mr Barnes says, pointing to one corner.

Cameron watches as a family of chickens stroll across the pitch.

"Well, where else would you keep your chickens?" Mr Barnes jokes.

After the village, the landscape is made up of farms and trees until they reach the volcano range and the view is filled with dark peaks reaching up into the sky.

Antonio explains, "The volcanoes make the soil rich, which is good for growing coffee. They also provide the necessary elevation, as coffee only grows at least 4000 feet above sea level."

As they arrive, Antonio explains they are going to see a finca. It is a small plantation, which produces a modest harvest and employs a handful of people.

The finca has the feel of a wild west ranch. There is a wooden bar above the access road with the name of the family carved into it. Beyond that, a farmhouse built from wood, looks out over the fields of coffee plants. In the distance, there are horses grazing.

Antonio invites the group to sit around a table strewn with berries and beans, before explaining the harvesting process. He picks up some red berries and shows them to everyone.

"These are coffee cherries," he explains. "First we must remove the fleshy part."

He places the 'cherries' back on the table and holds up a waxy bean.

"Then we dry the bean for at least 2 days."

Now he holds up a bean that looks old and withered.

"Next, we can remove the papery layer."

He rubs the bean between his thumb and

forefinger until the dried casing falls off. He is left with a small beige bean, which he passes around the group.

"As well as growing, drying and storing coffee, we also roast beans here. We have different roasts for you to try."

They follow Antonio inside, where he shows them an odd looking device. It has a wooden stand, holding a metal hoop supporting a cloth bag. He places a cup inside the stand and pours hot water into the cloth bag. A dark liquid starts to drip from the bag into the cup, and the smell of coffee fills the room.

"This is called a chorreador," Antonio tells them. "It is what we use to make coffee in Costa Rica."

There is a table with three urns of coffee for them to try. Antonio continues talking while they sample the different roasts.

"Coffee was introduced to Costa Rica in the early nineteenth century, and grew so well in our climate, the government offered free land to coffee farmers. The crop had potential to improve life for many ordinary people. Most people had small fincas but some were able to manage large plantations and employ many workers. They became rich and powerful members of society, and were known as the coffee barons."

Cameron considers what he has learned about coffee barons, while he drinks his coffee. Clearly Joselyn's family wasn't in that group, so it isn't likely there will be any history written about them that he can use to find the plantation. Possibly a greedy coffee baron tricked Andreas, stole his finca and made it part of their own plantation. A large plantation might still be in use. He would just need to find it.

"I know someone whose family used to grow coffee near Curubande. I wondered if there are still any plantations there?" he asks Antonio. "It might have been changed to a different kind of plantation since then."

"I'm sorry, I don't know of any plantations there, but that is near the Rincon de la Vieja volcano, so there certainly could be something in that area. It would probably have good soil," Antonio answers.

Cameron joins the queue to get back on the bus, thinking he is no closer to the answer he is looking for than when he got on it that morning. He does know a lot more about coffee though. And he thinks those coffee barons were not to be trusted.

He is determined to get some useful

information from this trip, though, and heads back to ask Antonio another question.

"Can you tell me what something means in English?" he asks. "It's La Plantacion en las Nubes. I think it's the plantation in the... something."

"That means the clouds," Antonio translates. "The Plantation in the Clouds. That would be a good name for a coffee plantation because coffee only grows at high elevations."

Cameron thinks about this. He knows the plantation was near Curubande and must have been high up in the hills, so it probably wasn't flooded. But at least now he knows who owned it, when they were there, and roughly where that was.

The bus has just started to move off when Cameron notices a large animal on the ground, at the edge of some trees. It looks like a giant brown badger, with an upright tail, like a lemur.

"What is that?" he wonders out loud.

Mr Barnes leans across the aisle, looks at the animal and raises his eyebrows.

"No idea. Where's Arthur when you need him?" he teases.

"Hey, Antonio, what's that animal?" Cameron calls out.

Antonio looks out of the window.

"That's a coati," he says. "It's like a large raccoon. It is a common animal here."

Everyone on the bus stares in wonder until the 'common' coati is no longer in sight.

By the time they get back to the hotel, Mr and Mrs Barnes have a plan for the remaining few hours of the afternoon. There are only two days left of the trip and they want to buy something to take home as a reminder. There are plenty of shops close to the hotel, offering a wide selection of souvenirs. They find books, jewellery, T-shirts, baseball caps, cuddly toys and chorreadors.

Mrs Barnes spends a long time pointedly looking at jewellery but Mr Barnes buys a book about the geography of Costa Rica. Cameron glances at their purchase; it looks... educational.

He chooses a T-shirt, the colour of the sea, with the words 'Costa Rica' emblazoned across the front. He takes it to the desk to pay.

Everything is priced in US Dollars here. Cameron works out roughly how much it costs in Costa Rican Colones, but it is a huge number. The prices seem to be twice as high as at the craft market. He knows he has a lot of coins but isn't sure if he has enough for the T-shirt. It will take a long time to count it all, and it will be embarrassing if he doesn't have enough, so he pays with a note.

The assistant hands him his change, and he stuffs these coins into his wallet, with all the others he has gained during the holiday. He is struggling to close it now. He knows he will have to spend his change before he leaves or it will be wasted; it probably won't be worth enough to cover the cost of exchanging it for English money when he gets home.

Home - that's not something he wants to think about right now. He puts his wallet back in his pocket as they head to the room for a well-deserved rest before dinner.

The balcony is quiet and has comfortable chairs. Cameron and Mr Barnes relax there with a cold drink, while Mrs Barnes responds to some emails inside.

As the sun sets, the cicadas start their nightly chorus.

"Look, I just saw one jump!" says Mr Barnes.

"Where?" asks Cameron, squinting to see better in the low light.

"I can't see it now."

Mr Barnes scans the edge of the forest but the cicadas are only visible when they move.

"I'm sorry, you missed it. I don't know where it went," he says.

"Story of my life," Cameron says, thinking aloud, "or is it? I know where Andreas went. If there's no record of his plantation where he came from, maybe there's something where he ended up!"

Mr Barnes frowns, confused by this strange turn in the conversation.

"Who's Andreas?"

Eleven

The White City

A taxi ride into the city and Cameron is ready to unearth some secrets.

"I wasn't expecting you to be so interested in a museum," Mrs Barnes says, as they walk the final few minutes to their destination - the Museum of Guanacaste.

"I thought you would have liked the Gold Museum better. I mean, it's full of gold," Mr Barnes says, clearly wishing they were in San Jose instead of Liberia.

"San Jose is a long way to travel," Mrs Barnes says. "I'm just impressed we've got him to a museum at all!"

"It's nice here," Cameron says. "Look at these lovely old buildings and wide streets, and oh..."

He stops speaking as they turn a corner and see the museum. It looks like a huge stone fort, or possibly a prison.

They buy tickets, collect their information sheet and step inside. Mr Barnes immediately starts reading the information.

"This building used to be a military headquarters and an armoury," he reads aloud. "Well, that explains its cheery appearance."

They wander through the rooms, each as unwelcoming as the last. Mr Barnes stops frequently to read information about the exhibits. Mrs Barnes is clearly hoping to leave soon and gives each case a cursory glance before moving on. Cameron is beginning to think this might not have been his best idea, when he spots a familiar looking artefact.

It is a wheel from an oxcart, just like the one at Rosa's house. He walks closer and sees that it is almost exactly like the one at Rosa's house. It has the same pattern of leaves radiating from a central metal plate. The colours are similar, too, though not exactly the same. It looks like it could have been made by Andreas.

There is a plaque with information about the exhibit, including an English translation. The exhibit is about early transportation in Costa Rica, including oxcarts. There are pages from the journal of a wheel maker named... Andreas. This can't be a coincidence!

Cameron looks around for help but there is no-one else in the room. He takes out his phone and takes a photo of the pages from the journal to show Joselyn. But he can't wait until he sees her - he needs to know what it says right now.

Fuelled by his determination to finish this story before he runs out of time, he rushes through the museum, looking in each room for a security guard to ask for help. The fortress it is housed in seems to be considered enough protection as Cameron can't locate anyone. He is certain he wouldn't have this problem at the Gold Museum. They must have plenty of security guards.

But then he sees them; not exactly what he was looking for, but an opportunity he can't refuse. There, in a room full of archeological finds, are a couple of young women. They both have cameras and sunglasses, and appear to be tourists, like him.

Both women have dark hair but quite light skin. One is wearing a stylish wide-brimmed sunhat and the other has an expensive-looking charm bracelet. He guesses they are European, which means they probably speak English well. He's not sure what they are saying but it sounds like Spanish, although it could be Portuguese or possibly Italian. He approaches them cautiously.

"Perdone," Cameron starts, but then realises he doesn't know enough Spanish to ask for what he needs.

"Do you speak English?" he asks instead.

"Yes," the lady in the hat answers.

"And, er, do you speak Spanish too?"

"Si," she replies.

Cameron knows this means 'yes'.

"Great! There's a journal in one of the cases back there that I'd really like to read."

He points to the rooms behind him before continuing his explanation.

"It's in Spanish, and there's no translation. I was wondering if you could tell me what it says?"

The kind tourists follow him back through the museum to the case housing the journal. Only a couple of the pages are visible, and Cameron really hopes they say something important. Although, he knows that if it is a complete waste of time, at least he is very unlikely to ever see these people again.

He points at the pages, and the lady in the hat starts to read aloud.

"It says: After falling into the Colorado River and losing all my money in its waters, I have abandoned my plantation and come to start a new life in the White City. I have secured a job working for a cart-maker, and have discovered a talent for painting oxcart wheels. Despite my sad reason for leaving home, I am hopeful that one day I may start my own business, and build a new life here."

She looks at him to signify she has finished reading. Cameron is about to thank her, when her friend points to an article that has been displayed alongside the journal.

"This says he became a prominent businessman in Liberia, and later married and had four children," the friend explains.

"That's brilliant, thank you, it's exactly what I needed to know!" Cameron gushes.

The two women smile as they walk away. They don't understand why a Costa Rican museum exhibit about an oxcart maker could be so important to a British boy, but he doesn't care. He has found Andreas. His reputation as a mystery-solver is validated.

He thinks about what this new information means. Andreas wasn't tricked, he literally lost his money in the river, like the person who dropped the coin Cameron picked up on the river trip. It was just an accident.

Cameron doesn't know what the White City part means though. He decides to look around the museum some more and see if there is anything that explains this new clue.

He enters another room and there it is, right above his head: a huge banner saying La Ciudad Blanca. He doesn't speak a lot of Spanish but he knows what that says - The White City. He reads the information by the door.

LIBERIA WAS CALLED THE 'WHITE CITY' BECAUSE OF THE WHITE GRAVEL AND WHITEWASHED HOUSES THAT WERE FOUND IN MUCH OF THE TOWN.

That makes sense, he thinks. Andreas lost his money in the Colorado River, near a place called Curubande. According to the map of the region he looked at before, Curubande is not that far from Liberia.

So he made his way to the city to look for work, and became an oxcart wheel-maker. Whatever happened to the plantation, he never went back there. 170 years later, his family is still in the White City.

Twelve

The Table Tennis Truce

"Yes!" Cameron exclaims loudly. "Day off," he explains to his startled parents.

His calendar app tells him he has no more trips booked for the remainder of the holiday, which he is really happy about, because after all the treks and hikes and uncomfortable coach journeys, he needs a rest. He has the meet up with Joselyn at the beach tomorrow and he can't wait to tell her the news about Andreas.

If only he knew what had happened to the plantation as well. At least he hadn't promised to solve the mystery. She will probably be less disappointed than he is.

He rubs on some sun cream and head down to the pool with his parents. It is a very large pool and the water is an inviting shade of turquoise blue. There are built-in loungers on a raised level in the shallow end. They look very appealing.

The pool is surrounded by a tiered terrace with each level providing plentiful sun loungers and shade. Mr and Mrs Barnes settle in with their books. Cameron drops off his towel and makes his way to the pool.

He swims for a few minutes, then tries one of the loungers in the pool. It is very comfortable and relaxing. He worries he might actually fall asleep and get sunburnt, so he rejoins his parents and relaxes on a lounger in the shade instead.

"Hi!"

Arthur appears out of nowhere just as Cameron is at his most vulnerable. He sits up with a start.

"Where did you come from?" he asks, sounding more annoyed than he meant to.

He doesn't look over at his dad, who he already knows is frowning at him.

"I was looking for you," Arthur says. "I thought you might like to play table tennis with me."

"Er..." Cameron says, trying to think of a reason why he can't possibly play table tennis right now.

"That's a great idea," Mr Barnes says. "You always get bored lazing by the pool."

Cameron looks around, hoping to see someone else around Arthur's age, who might actually want to play with him. There is no-one.

"Yeah, OK, let's play," he says.

Arthur's expression transforms into an enormous smile, as if this is the best thing anyone has ever said to him. Cameron sighs and puts his trainers back on, while Arthur lets his parents know where he's going.

"Go easy on him," Mrs Barnes says to Cameron.

"I'll try," Cameron lies.

The table tennis table is unfortunately free. Arthur knows the rules, but is not very sporty and concedes almost every point. Cameron usually enjoys winning but winning in three minutes flat is just boring.

"Thanks for the game," he says turning to leave.

"That wasn't very long," Arthur says. "Could we have another one?"

"Well, I was planning to go for a swim," Cameron says.

"It's just that I don't really have any other friends here..."

This hangs between them for a moment, while Cameron considers how to respond.

"Ok, let's have another game. Maybe you can get some points this time!"

Arthur laughs, really not caring how badly he

loses. After beating Arthur three games in a row, Cameron decides he has babysat long enough.

"I'm going back to my room to play some games," he says.

"Can I come with you? I'll be quiet."

Cameron doubts this very much. He doesn't have any other plans until lunchtime, though, and Arthur seems happy just to have someone to spend time with. Without any agreement, Arthur runs off to tell his parents where he is going. Cameron sighs and starts walking. The kid can catch up.

In the room, Cameron uses the code his parents gave him to retrieve his tablet from the safe, and starts a game. Arthur picks up the geography book his parents bought the previous day and flicks through the pages.

"It says here bananas can grow at just 600 metres above sea level," he says.

"Really," Cameron replies, not paying attention.

Then, what Arthur has said sinks in.

"Wait, what?"

"Bananas grow at elevations above 600 metres up to a maximum of 1800 metres," he reads aloud.

"So, a coffee plantation couldn't have been turned into a banana plantation, then?"

"I don't know. Why did you ask that?"

"Oh, you remember I told you about my friend whose family used to have a coffee plantation. It was called La Plantacion en las Nubes."

"The plantation in the...?"

"Clouds."

"So that must have been quite high up then. Well, it probably says in here."

Arthur turns the pages of the book until he finds a section about coffee.

"Don't bother," Cameron replies. "I know all about coffee. It only grows at least 4000 feet above sea level."

"Hmm, let's see. So we need to change feet into metres. There are approximately 3 feet in a metre, so that makes..."

Cameron closes his game and searches for a measurement converter website instead.

"It's 1220 metres."

"So it is possible," Arthur says, with his usual cheerfulness.

"I don't think they would have called the place 'the plantation in the clouds' if it was the minimum height above sea level. It is possible, but unlikely." Cameron sighs loudly. "That was my last idea."

He puts down the tablet and stares at the wall. Arthur studies the book in silence.

"There are some cool pictures of volcanoes erupting in here," he says, holding the book in front of Cameron. "I would like to see an eruption in real life but from a safe distance."

Cameron doesn't respond, so Arthur carries on talking.

"They have good names, too. Tenorio, Miravalles, Orosi..."

"OK, I get it," Cameron interrupts.

He is not keen to hear the name of every single volcano in the country. Arthur is engrossed and continues regardless.

"Arenal - we've seen that one! Also, Rincon de la Vieja..."

"Wait, what does it say about that one?

"Only that it doesn't erupt anymore."

Cameron sighs again.

"It used to erupt a lot, though."

Cameron tries to remember when Joselyn said her family had lost the plantation. Was it the 1850s?

"I don't suppose it erupted around the middle to late nineteenth century, did it?" he asks, trying to sound casual.

He has the feeling this could actually be really important.

"Loads, it erupted from 1853 to 1854, again in 1860, then from 1861 all the way to 1863..."

"What kind of eruptions are we talking about?" Cameron asks. "Lava burning everything in its path and ash clouds blocking out the sunlight, or a few fireworks and a bit of smoke?"

He is giving Arthur his complete attention now.

"It says 'phreatic eruptions'," Arthur replies.

Cameron grabs his tablet again and starts another web search.

"That means it rained rocks and spewed deadly toxic gas. That doesn't sound good. Even without any lava flow, the surrounding area would have been poisoned. Any plantations nearby would have been ruined!"

"And people would have had to flee, just like around Arenal," Arthur adds.

"So it doesn't matter what happened to make the family lose the plantation, because losing it probably saved their lives. Even if they had survived, the land would have been worthless. No crop could have grown on it for years."

Cameron sits down on the bed and exhales slowly as a disturbing thought forms in his mind. If Great, Great, Great-Grandfather Andreas hadn't fallen in a river all those years ago, Joselyn wouldn't exist!

He looks across at the kid he has spent most of the week trying to avoid.

"Thanks, Arthur. You've been really helpful."

Arthur just smiles. It hadn't entered his head that Cameron might ever have thought otherwise.

Thirteen

Hidden Treasure

On the last day of the holiday, Cameron meets Joselyn and her friend outside his hotel, for a relaxing day at the beach.

"This is Fabola," Joselyn says, introducing a girl with black hair and eyes nearly as dark.

Fabola grins and says, "Hi. I've heard a lot about you."

"Let's check the flag," says Joselyn, before Cameron can ask exactly what Fabola has heard.

"The flag?" he asks.

"To see if it's safe to swim."

It is just a short walk to the beach, which is right behind the hotel. The sand is a dull greyish-beige colour but very soft. Their pace slows as their feet sink a little with each step. Cameron stops and takes his trainers off.

"Watch out for the crabs!" Fabola calls,

playfully.

Cameron laughs, but then sees a tiny crab scuttle across the sand, not far from his feet.

"Thanks for the warning," he calls back to her.

He catches up with the girls, who are looking down the beach at a little green flag waving in the breeze.

"It's safe," Fabola sighs. "We have no excuse to be completely lazy all day."

"Well, actually," Cameron begins, "I do need to use up my change. I was thinking maybe I could get us all some ice-cream later. There's a little shop I saw yesterday that's just up the road."

"Sounds like a great idea," Joselyn says.

"I can see why you like him," Fabola teases her.

Joselyn narrows her eyes, in an expression she hopes conveys annoyance, but as usual she just looks cute.

They agree on a spot to leave their bags while they are in the water. The girls remove their dresses and leave them with their bags. Fabola is wearing a black swimming costume and Joselyn is wearing a sporty blue bikini. Cameron feels a bit weird being half-naked with two girls. He tries not to look at them, until they are all in the sea.

The sand may be dull, but the sea is a bright

aqua-green, becoming more turquoise further from the shore, as it gets deeper. Despite her joke about being lazy, Fabola is soon swimming, with Joselyn following her closely. Cameron takes a few minutes to acclimatise to the cool temperature of the water, slowly walking into the sea until the water is up to his waist, before starting to swim. He is a strong swimmer and catches them up quickly.

Soon, they are splashing each other and playing tag in the sea, as if they have known each other for years. The girls shriek each time they are tagged or splashed, and Cameron laughs so much he soon needs a rest. They head back to their towels and dry off. In a few minutes they are hot again.

"There's something I wanted to tell you," Cameron begins.

The girls turn their attention to him, and he hopes his news will be well-received.

"I was trying to find out what happened to your family's plantation. I found something in the Museum of Guanacaste about Andreas. He wrote a journal and they have it there. It says he fell in the river and lost all his money so he had to leave the plantation and move to the city."

"Wow, so he didn't gamble away his money or get tricked by a coffee baron then," Joselyn says. "I wonder how long that exhibit has been there. The museum is not far from where I live but I've never been inside."

"Also, I didn't find out exactly where the plantation was," Cameron continues, "but I did found out the area above Curubande was covered by burning rocks and toxic gas from the volcano, several times in the 1850's and 60's."

Joselyn is staring at him intently.

"You mean..."

"If Andreas hadn't lost the plantation, he could have died in a volcanic eruption. Even if he had survived, the plantation would have been ruined."

They all sit in silence for a moment, taking this in, until it starts to feel awkward.

"So, about that ice-cream..." Fabola says.

After putting on their clothes, they make their way to the shop Cameron spotted the day before. It is one of those places with someone serving ice-cream from an open-top freezer at the front. The flavours look fairly similar to those you can buy in the UK, and some of the names are similar too. Coco must be coconut, Cameron thinks, and chocolate is called chocolate here, too. There are a few types he isn't sure about, which Fabola explains are fruits grown in the area.

Joselyn chooses coconut. Fabola chooses a fruit called Granadilla and lets Cameron try some, before he chooses. It tastes like passionfruit, which he likes, but he still chooses chocolate. Joselyn takes his ice-cream so he can pay.

Tipping all the coins from his wallet into his hand to count out the amount he needs, he struggles to find the correct change because all the coins look the same. They come in slightly different sizes but all have the same picture on one side - the Costa Rica coat of arms. He has to turn some of them over so they all have the side showing the amount facing upwards, to see how much they are worth.

Fabola stifles a giggle at his slow progress, and Joselyn frowns at her.

"Here, hold these," he says tipping the coins into Fabola's free hand. "I can't read this one - it's too dirty."

He realises this must be the coin he picked up at the river. He didn't get round to cleaning it properly. He wipes it on his T-shirt and looks for the amount. It's just a one, but wait... it says a different currency on it.

"Oh, no, I think this one isn't even Costa Rican!"

He laughs, holding it up for the girls to see.

"Look, it says Escudo."

He places the coin on the counter and Joselyn leans in to take a closer look. Cameron starts taking coins from Fabola's hand and passing them to the store assistant, who counts them really quickly and tells him how much more he needs. Cameron counts out more, slowly, until he has paid enough. When he finishes, he turns to the girls who are staring at him.

"I know, I took ages and the ice-cream has melted," he laughs, taking his ice-cream and licking a drip that is about to fall.

"This coin you have - we learned about these in school. It is a gold Escudo from 1850, one of the first coins ever minted with the Costa Rica coat of arms. It's really rare," Joselyn explains.

"And valuable," Fabola adds, excitedly.

Cameron takes a moment to process this information. He looks at the coin again, then looks back at the girls. He has to decide what to do with it and there isn't much time before he leaves the country.

"You're rich! You should keep it," urges Fabola.

"You could donate it to the National Museum - it's a treasure of our country," Joselyn suggests, "But it's yours, so you should decide."

Cameron thinks for a moment, and then hands

the coin to Joselyn. Fabola rolls her eyes.

"You know she's going to give that to the museum, don't you?" she says.

Joselyn smiles and says, "Hundreds of years ago, the Spanish came looking for gold - and they missed the real treasure."

Cameron looks puzzled, unsure what she means by this.

"Real treasure?"

"What has been worth the most to you on this trip?" she asks.

"Well, I guess the best parts have been the experiences I never had before - being in the rainforest at night, going high up in the cloud forest canopy, being kept awake up by howler monkeys, and well, you know, like... meeting you," he mumbles.

He stares down at the ground, expecting to be relentlessly teased for this uncharacteristic show of sentimentality.

"Exactly," is her gentle reply.

Ciudad de Guanacaste
October 1850

Andreas liked the city; he liked all the people he saw every day, he liked that there was always something happening, and he liked how the white stone-covered roads reflected the sunlight making everything look bright and cheerful.

He tried not to think about how he had been forced to abandon the plantation because he couldn't afford to pay the bills. That dream was over, he had a new life now, painting oxcart wheels. He enjoyed painting the intricate designs on them - each one just a little bit different - and he felt happy when people appreciated his work, or bought a set of wheels because they thought their friends would admire them.

This day was market day, the day he did not make wheels to be fitted to the carts that the business owner sold from his shop, but instead took his favourite creations to the market to sell. He never took his very first wheel, the one with the pattern of leaves radiating from the centre. Once he had earned enough to start his own business, it would be going on the wall of his own workshop.

It had been a good day with several sales but the light was beginning to fade, so he packed up the cart with his remaining merchandise.

As he was just about to climb onto the seat, someone spoke.

"Such beautiful wheels - did you make them yourself?"

Andreas turned to see a young woman in a pale dress, standing beside the cart.

"I paint them. I work for the cart-maker on the main street," he replied.

The woman smiled and reached out to touch one of the wheels.

"I'm sorry, I don't need a cart, or any wheels, I just thought they were lovely. But you are packing up to go, I won't take up any more of your time."

"It's getting dark," Andreas said quickly, not wanting her to leave. "I could see you home, if you like."

"That's very kind of you - but don't you have to return the cart?" the woman asked.

"The workshop is not far, I could return this in a few minutes and walk you home. You could see the workshop, if you are interested."

"I'd like that," she replied. "My name is Camila."

"I'm Andreas."

He held out his hand, to help Camila onto the seat of the oxcart. As her hand touched his, he felt a strange familiarity, although he was sure they hadn't met before. Uncertainly, he climbed onto the seat next to her and tried not to look across as the ox slowly plodded back to the barn where it would spend the night.

Andreas unhitched the ox and locked up the cart quickly, as he didn't want to leave his new friend waiting in the twilight for too long. As they began the walk to her home, he found himself hoping she didn't live close by. She led him through the streets into a quieter area at the edge of the city, chatting about her home and family as they walked.

A snuffling sound behind them made them both look back, but there were fewer houses in this part of town so not enough light to see what had made the noise.

"I hope it is only El Cadejo," Camila joked.

"I was saved by El Cadejo once," Andreas replied.

He didn't really believe that, but it made a good story.

"I would love to hear about that!" Camila said. "Come over for dinner tomorrow and you can tell me what happened."

They reached her home, where someone had lit a lantern on the porch. As she turned to say goodnight, the light illuminated her golden brown hair and hazel eyes. For a moment, the sight took Andreas' breath away. He left reluctantly, promising to return the next day.

He knew he would keep that promise, because of the idea that grew with every step, that he was somehow supposed to lose the plantation. He felt like one chapter of his story had finished but another was just beginning.

Glancing back towards Camila's house, he had the strongest feeling he was exactly where he was meant to be.

Thank You

Thank you for reading this book! I hope you enjoyed it.

You can help other readers discover my books by leaving a short review on Amazon, Goodreads, or Bookbub. It would mean the world to me.

Deborah

Author's Note

In Spanish, where an exclamation mark or question mark is used, it is shown inverted (upside down) at the beginning of the sentence, as well as the usual way up at the end. There are also accent marks over some of the letters. As the majority of this text is in English, I have used only English punctuation.

All the places in this story are real. The characters are my own creations. The rivers that roll down from the volcano range in Guanacaste, including the Rio Colorado, flow to the Rio Tempisque, depositing debris in its waters. In the dry season, things can be washed up on the banks of the Tempisque, but people tend not to search for treasure in this area because of the large population of crocodiles.

The Ciudad de Guanacaste was once known as the White City but has been known as Liberia since 1854. It is now a thriving city with an international airport.

If you visit Costa Rica, you will be able to see a volcano, swim in hot springs, encounter nocturnal creatures in the rainforest, see monkey bridges, cross hanging bridges in the canopy of the cloud forest, visit a hacienda, get up close and personal with crocodiles, learn how to grow and harvest coffee, hear some unusual folklore and see a lot of oxcart wheels.

Or you could have a completely different adventure.

Bonus Chapter

Want to know what happened in Chesil beach, south coast of England, in 1381? Here's the first chapter of The Lost Cargo, book three of The Lost Mysteries.

At first, it was just moving a few bales of woollen cloth late at night. Every year, a man from the next village came to shear the sheep. Packing the wool into jute sacks and loading them onto the cart was one of Gregory's duties. The last summer, the man had kept aside a few wool packs for himself. Gregory hadn't said anything to Sir Walter. A couple of days later, one of the other farmhands had asked if he would be interested in some extra work. That was how it had started.

They just needed a man to take the cloth down to the beach in the night. The master wouldn't miss it, there was more than enough, after all. It turned out Gregory was good at hiding in the dark and moving things unseen.

The bales were collected by someone from a ship heading into Exmouth on legitimate business. The ship would wait a little way offshore while a crewman came in a rowboat and picked up the cargo. Gregory left the wool on the tall bank of pebbles that formed the start of the shingle beach. He placed the packs on the side facing away from the sea, where they would not be seen by customs officers checking the area for smugglers. The officers weren't particularly menacing, most were smaller and weaker than him, but they kept watch in pairs or small groups, knowing how resistant the locals were to their demands.

If it wasn't safe to land the boat, Gregory had to call out and alert the receiver. It was easy enough for him to hide in the darkness to evade capture. If it came to it, he would simply throw pebbles at the officers before making a run for it. So far, such a situation had never occurred but it was always a good idea to have a back-up plan.

As long as it was safe for them to come ashore, he only needed to check that someone came to collect the cloth. He would wait until the rowboat arrived, then roll the bales down the bank, and leave. It wasn't part of the arrangement to help them load it into the boat.

Gregory sometimes questioned his choice. If caught, he would most likely be sent to prison and could lose his family's home, or more accurately, the place where his family lived. The house was owned by Sir Walter, like all the other land and property around the village. Being a serf tied to Sir Walter's land meant he couldn't leave the manor, or take work from anyone else, and he could only rent land to grow his crops. If he was caught, there would only be his wife, Cathy, bringing in money, and she was barely paid enough to keep herself fed.

On the other hand, if he kept his head down and

became a favourite at the big house, Sir Walter might one day make him a villein. He would have his own land, and only be expected to work for the master at the busiest times of year. That might have been enough for him but his children deserved a better life. So the smuggling continued.

As time went on, Gregory's list of duties grew. Most often, he collected the shipments coming in from France or Holland. Sometimes it was tea, sometimes wine, occasionally it would be fine lace that had taken someone months to make. A waste of time in his opinion, but as long as they paid for it, he brought the tubs in and kept his mouth shut. That was his job tonight - to collect whatever was coming in.

It was important to pay close attention to the weather. The winds were often dangerous; ships were sometimes wrecked and people on the beach had been swept out to sea. He hunched over, both to shield his tall body from the cold wind and to keep from being seen. Conditions could change very quickly so it was best to be careful.

A light in the distance signalled the ship had arrived. Gregory looked both ways along the beach. Visibility was only about ten metres on a cloudy night so he listened, too. Nothing. If there was anyone there, he would have heard them; walking on the loose pebbles of the shingle beach made a lot of noise.

He stepped slowly towards the small wooden boat he had moved closer to the water earlier that evening. It belonged to a man in the village called Rowan who ferried goods to and from the island. Although the shingle bank ran all the way to Portland, making a causeway connecting the island to the mainland, anyone needing to take anything heavy there would require a boat. People didn't often need to take anything heavy to the island so this boat was used infrequently, and it was unlikely the owner would notice it had been borrowed. He probably wouldn't report it, even if its use was noticed.

Taxes were high so everyone understood why people smuggled, and no-one liked the customs men anyway. They worked for the child who was on the throne - Richard II; the one who said he would end serfdom and give everyone their freedom and then changed his mind. The one keeping Gregory and his family and friends stuck in that village for the rest of their lives, working hard for someone else and never having anything for themselves.

Besides, Gregory talked with Rowan in the street sometimes. He often regaled the farmworkers with tales of interesting places. Most of the villagers had never been anywhere so the stories were always popular. Rowan reckoned from the top of the hill on Portland, you could see all the way to Lyme Regis. Gregory had never been that far in his life so didn't know if it was even true but he wanted to believe it.

There had been a story about a cave too, where smugglers sometimes hid things they didn't want anyone else to find. Maybe one day he would go to Portland and find that cave. One day, when his time was his own.

With some effort, he launched the boat into the sea and climbed inside, taking the oars. Small waves pushed back against the modest craft as he rowed out to meet the ship. This brought to mind the first time he had seen a ship up close; the size of it had been astonishing. Viewed from the village, passing vessels looked much smaller than they really were. In reality, they were as big as all the workers' houses in the village put together, rising several metres above the water, with sails reaching up into the sky. There was no time to appreciate the impressive sight tonight though, there was a job to be done.

He didn't usually have any contact with the crew. On a normal night, they dropped the tubs into the sea and moved away quickly. They knew someone was out there in the darkness, waiting until they were out of sight before moving in to collect the cargo. Until that night he had done the special job, none of the ships' crews had ever spoken to him or seen his face. To get his payment, he would have to be seen again.

Approaching the ship, Gregory looked over his shoulder to see the tubs being dropped into the water by two large, bearded men. He continued towards them, slowing as the boat got closer. One of the men saw him and moved out of sight, causing his heart to beat a little faster. After a few seconds, an object was lowered over the side of the ship. Gregory reached up and grabbed it, quickly untying the rope so it could be pulled back up.

"Thank you," he called up to the strangers.

He didn't speak French but expected they would know a bit of English from their dealings with the port authorities and the locals in the nearby inns. There wasn't usually any need for conversation during the collections but they were taking a big risk too, and it wouldn't have felt right not to say something.

The possibility that the incentive of a special payment wouldn't actually be fulfilled had crossed Gregory's mind. As everything had been arranged through an intermediary, the name of the client was kept secret. If they hadn't followed through on their promise, there wasn't much a farm labourer could do about it.

Such a risky assignment wouldn't normally have been given a moment's consideration but Gregory's son, Peter, had just turned 10. It wouldn't be long before the boy would start working for Sir Walter and that would be his life, every day until he died. Little Elspeth would follow soon after. Gregory couldn't stand the thought of his sweet girl being worn down by servitude. He would do whatever it took to buy their freedom.

After placing the box under the bench, he set about collecting the tubs from the sea as the ship continued her journey. It was hard to lift the wet barrels and these were particularly heavy but his rough hands gave him a firm grip. From the weight, it seemed the cargo was wine this time. Having done manual work since his teenage years - ploughing and planting and harvesting in the fields - Gregory was strong enough for this job. They needed a reliable person and rewarded him fairly for the work. He was comforted by the knowledge that no self-important landowning lord was getting rich from his night-time endeavours.

Getting the cargo back to shore was the easy part. Hauling it over the shingle bank was back-breaking work, yet it didn't seem so hard this time. Once they were over the top of the bank, the barrels could be rolled down the other side. At the bottom, there were ropes to tie them together and sacks of pebbles ready to weight them, if needed. Then all he had to do was push them into the lagoon. Someone else would collect them in a few days, when they could no longer be linked to the ship's arrival. There was talk of a tunnel used for transporting smuggled cargo, but its exact location was a closely guarded secret.

Gregory returned to the boat once more to retrieve the box. Taking out the item inside and unwrapping the cloth cover, he could barely identify his emotions. A warm feeling spread through his chest, making his back straighten and his chin lift a little. This reward was very valuable, and one thought kept repeating in his mind: he had earned it.

Pride - that was what he was feeling. He hadn't felt pride in a very long time.

He placed the payment in a spare sack and carried it over his shoulder, checking along his route to avoid anyone else who might be out at that time. He was good at hiding in the dark and moving things unseen but this night he took extra care.

Glossary

Adios	Spanish for 'goodbye'
Amigo	Spanish for 'friend'
Ayudeme	Spanish for 'help me'
Bien	Spanish for 'nice'
Bueno	Spanish for 'good'
El Cadejo	Mythical huge, red-eyed dog from Costa Rican folklore
Caiman	An amphibious carnivore, related to the alligator
La Careta Sin Bueyes	Mythical oxcart without oxen from Costa Rican folklore
Chorreador	A traditional coffee maker
Cicada	A large nocturnal insect with a repetitive call
Coati	Large member of the raccoon family that lives in forests

Colon	Unit of currency in Costa Rica
Cordillera	Range of volcanoes
Escudo	Former unit of currency in Costa Rica
Esta	Spanish for 'this is'
Finca	Small family-owned farm
Geothermal Energy	Heat from inside the Earth is used to turn water into steam, which turns turbines, to make electricity
Gracias	Spanish for 'thank you'
Hacienda	Large plantation house
Hola	Spanish for 'hello'
Hydropower	Energy converted from flowing water into electricity
Molasses	Called black treacle in the UK, this is produced during the sugar refining process
La Mona	Mythical witch monkey from Costa Rican folklore

Muy	Spanish for 'very', as used in 'muy bien', which means 'very nice'
Las Nubes	Spanish for 'the clouds'
Olingo	A mammal, related to the raccoon, that lives in trees
Patacones	Fried plantains - a member of the banana family
Perdone	Spanish for 'excuse me'
Plantation	A farm where crops are grown
Porcupine	Large rodent whose back is covered in spiny quills, similar to a hedgehog but greater in size
Pura Vida	Good life - a wish for health and vitality, used often in Costa Rica
Rio	Spanish for 'river'
Si	Spanish for 'yes'

Tamales	Hot corn bread filled with beans, meat or vegetables, cooked in a corn husk
Tortillas	Flatbreads

9 781671 897410